This Book Belongs To:

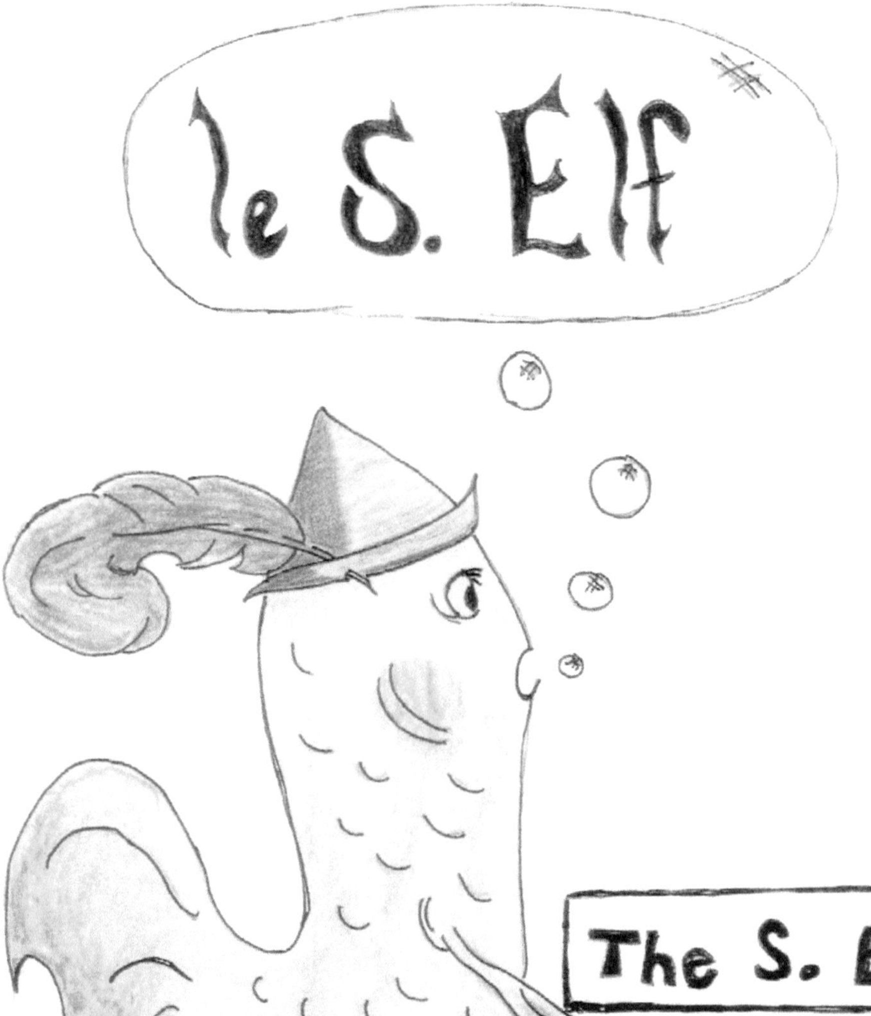

The S. Elf

By Lyle Erickson

Order this book online at www.trafford.com
or email orders@trafford.com

Most Trafford titles are also available at major online book retailers.

Trafford
PUBLISHING® www.trafford.com
North America & international
toll-free: 1 888 232 4444 (USA & Canada)
fax: 812 355 4082

Our mission is to efficiently provide the world's finest, most comprehensive book publishing service, enabling every author to experience success. To find out how to publish your book, your way, and have it available worldwide, visit us online at www.trafford.com

Because of the dynamic nature of the Internet, any web addresses or links contained in this book may have changed since publication and may no longer be valid. The views expressed in this work are solely those of the author and do not necessarily reflect the views of the publisher, and the publisher hereby disclaims any responsibility for them.

Any people depicted in stock imagery provided by Getty Images are models,
and such images are being used for illustrative purposes only.
Certain stock imagery © Getty Images.

ISBN: 978-1-6987-0240-7
ISBN: 978-1-6987-0239-1

Print information available on the last page.

Trafford rev. 07/31/2020

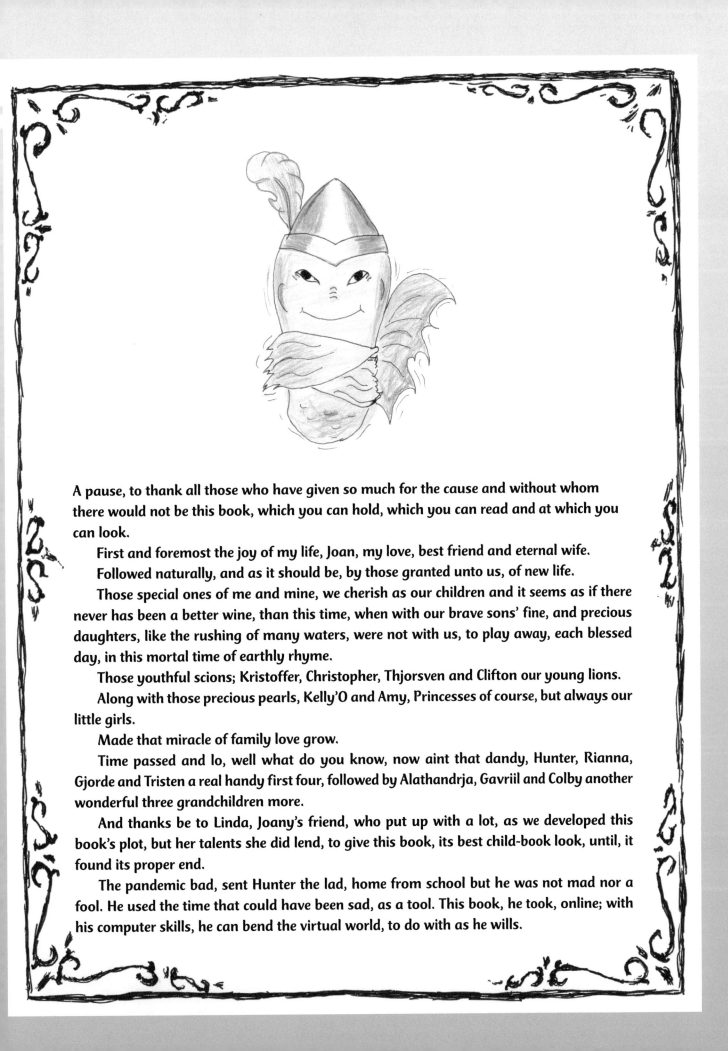

A pause, to thank all those who have given so much for the cause and without whom there would not be this book, which you can hold, which you can read and at which you can look.

First and foremost the joy of my life, Joan, my love, best friend and eternal wife.

Followed naturally, and as it should be, by those granted unto us, of new life.

Those special ones of me and mine, we cherish as our children and it seems as if there never has been a better wine, than this time, when with our brave sons' fine, and precious daughters, like the rushing of many waters, were not with us, to play away, each blessed day, in this mortal time of earthly rhyme.

Those youthful scions; Kristoffer, Christopher, Thjorsven and Clifton our young lions.

Along with those precious pearls, Kelly'O and Amy, Princesses of course, but always our little girls.

Made that miracle of family love grow.

Time passed and lo, well what do you know, now aint that dandy, Hunter, Rianna, Gjorde and Tristen a real handy first four, followed by Alathandrja, Gavriil and Colby another wonderful three grandchildren more.

And thanks be to Linda, Joany's friend, who put up with a lot, as we developed this book's plot, but her talents she did lend, to give this book, its best child-book look, until, it found its proper end.

The pandemic bad, sent Hunter the lad, home from school but he was not mad nor a fool. He used the time that could have been sad, as a tool. This book, he took, online; with his computer skills, he can bend the virtual world, to do with as he wills.

Le S. Elf Fish (THE SELFISH)

*TOUCHÉ (Too shay)

*Touché: used to acknowledge a hit in fencing or the success of an argument, an accusation, or a witty point.

THE END

*Le S. Elf (Luh Ess Elf) lived in a small, blue pond.

From which he NEVER.... EVER.... ventured beyond.

He lived, by himself, all.... alone.... there.

For with others.... Le S. Elf refused to share.

*The Elf

Bubble-Bubble, Glug-Glug.

Sang Le S. Elf so smug

As he gave himself a hug.

For him there was no "you and me".

No friends... no family.

He thought that if he were alone he would be happy.

In his heart, to himself, he cried..."Whoopee"!

All alone, by himself,

was he.

In this small, blue pond

he called a sea.

This is the way

he wanted things to be.

Bubble-Bubble, Glug-Glug.

Sang Le S. Elf so smug.

As he gave himself a hug.

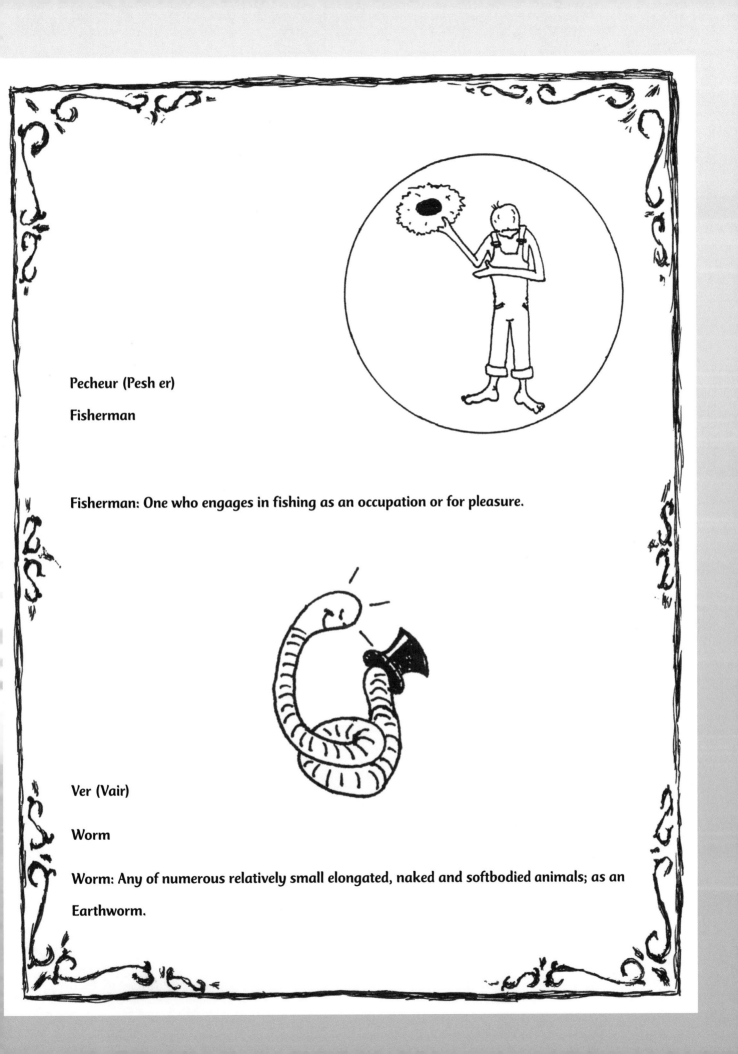

Pecheur (Pesh er)

Fisherman

Fisherman: One who engages in fishing as an occupation or for pleasure.

Ver (Vair)

Worm

Worm: Any of numerous relatively small elongated, naked and softbodied animals; as an

Earthworm.

Canard (Can-nar)

Duck

Duck: Any of various swimming, web-footed birds in which the neck and legs are short, the body depressed and the bill broad and flat.

Garconnet (Gar-sewn)

Boy

Boy: A male child, from birth to puberty.

One day.... a *Tortue de mer (tor-tue duh mare) came to stay.

Turtle moved.... very.... very.... slow.

He sank to the bottom of the pond.... deep.... down....low.

Like a mossy, old rock Tortue de mer did lay.

He had no desire for games of frolic or play.

Staying in the cool, deep water was what really made his day.

*Turtle

Le S. Elf gave a ferocious, fish-bubble gurgle.

His scales darkened, becoming a most annoying shade of purple.

A real thug at heart, he had been waiting so he could act tough.

He was certainly bad enough to be mean and rough.

Fiercely he huffed.

Savagely he puffed.

He knew he could call any other critter's bluff.

"T...h...i...i...s...s...s...s is MY pond.

Of you, Mr. Turtle, I am far less than fond.

Don't.. .you.. .dare.. .stay!

Tortue de mer...you must...you must....Go away."

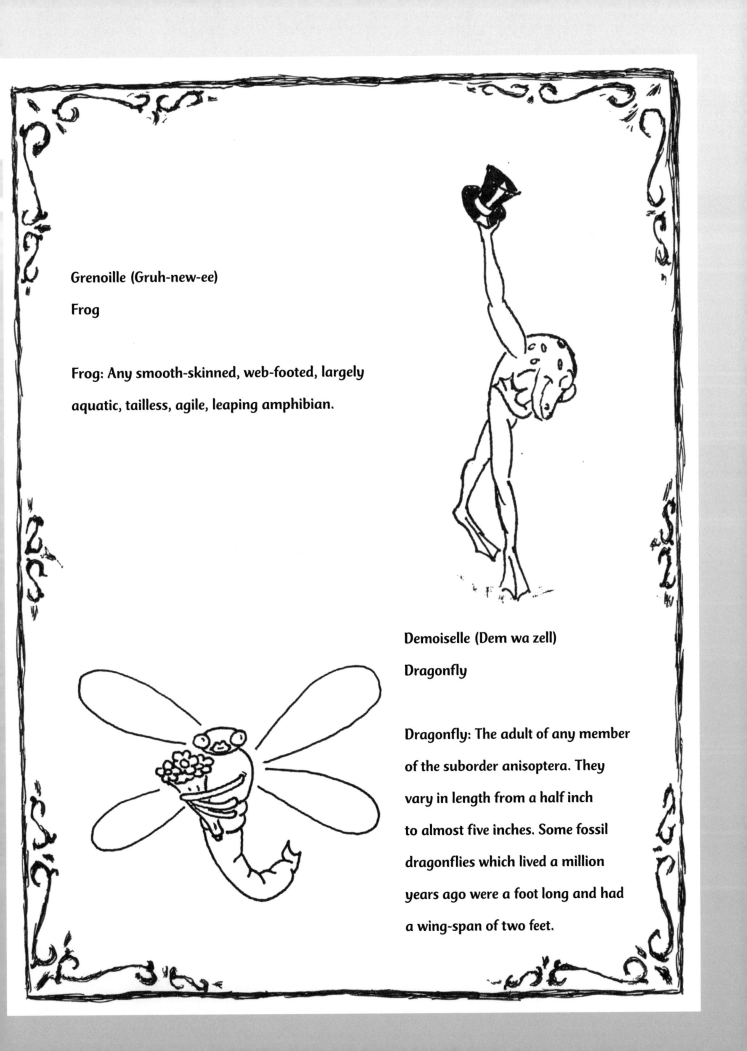

Grenoille (Gruh-new-ee)

Frog

Frog: Any smooth-skinned, web-footed, largely aquatic, tailless, agile, leaping amphibian.

Demoiselle (Dem wa zell)

Dragonfly

Dragonfly: The adult of any member of the suborder anisoptera. They vary in length from a half inch to almost five inches. Some fossil dragonflies which lived a million years ago were a foot long and had a wing-span of two feet.

CAST OF CHARACTERS AS THEY APPEAR IN THE STORY:

Le S. Elf *(Luh ess elf)*

The S. Elf

ELF: A small, mischievous or

malicious creature.

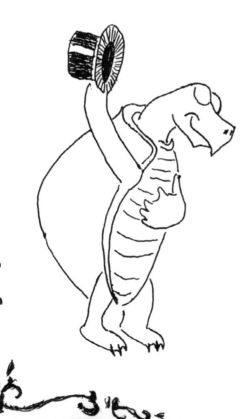

Tortue de mer *(Tor-tue duh mare)*

Turtle

Turtle: Any of an order of land,

fresh-water or marine reptiles that

has a toothless, bony beak and a

bony shell enclosing the trunk and

into which the head, limbs and tail

can be withdrawn.

Le S. Elf continued to bellow his most ferocious and loudest fish shout.

Telling poor, dowdy, old turtle how much he wanted him...OUT!

"Must I say it again... TURTLE... that you have to go?

Aha...then... let it be so! Turtle... I say...you really are very stupid and slow.

Now, turtle...don't...you...dare...give me no trouble.

Get out of here.. .stupid.. .slow one...on the double."

Poor Tortue de mer.

His tender heart became filled with a sudden, cold fear.

So.. .shedding.. .many.. .a.. .big...salt-tear,

Old mossy-rock turtle immediately departed.

All very sad and broken-hearted.

He went out into the cold and cruel
"Big Beyond."
Far and away from a cozy home
in the small blue pond.

A bright, shiny, green *Grenoille (gruh-new-ee) hopped.

You might say.. .he more or less.. .from out of the sky...dropped.

Whatever you choose to call it...at his coming he really just sort of...ker-plopped!

When into the pond he came with a bold, green dash.

Frog's sudden, unexpected, humongous crash

Was such a pond-shattering splash

That it made Le S. Elf's heart skip and fade

Just a thump...thump...thumpity...tad shade.

Le S. Elf curled his thin fish lips.

He even did a couple of

fast fish flips,

Tumbling right over

his own fine, fishy fin.

What a terrible fish

fit...this fish...

did fall

in.

*Frog

After all has been said and done,

It is a whole lot better and gobs more fun

Down on the small, blue water-world pond.

And...even out there in the big, Big, BIG beyond

Now that Le S. Elf-fish...(THE SELFISH)...is gone.

They all get along.

They sing a happy together-song.

Bubbly-bubble, glug-glug,

Be quick to give another a hug.

When you are willing to sh

There is room and plenty to

May there always be

laughter and mirth

All together, here

on our awesome...

big...blue Earth.

It was a not a juicy worm but the hard, metal hook...

That angry Le S. Elf suddenly took!

When, with a shout of fisherman's joy,

The red-headed, freckle-faced boy,

On his pole gave a yank and pull.

And Le S. Elf got his obnoxious, loud mouth full!

With a loud bubble-glug yell

That certainly did not sound at all well,

Le S. Elf chased green frog away...

Pell-mell

"Ooohh, swell!" Croaked gentleman frog

As he hopped out onto a log.

He would never be one to insist that he be allowed to stay.

But he was rather 'unsettled' at being told to go away.

And it was true, he realized,

That to this pond, as yet, he had no family ties.

Also...and most importantly...in the ways of the water world he was rather wise.

Grenoille was far too smart...and in no mood...

To become....FISH FOOD!!!!

Indeed, without waiting to even stop,

Except, of course, for that first...

big...splash ker-plop,

Proper...as proper could be...

away went frog in one, quick...

green...blur of a hop.

A wind-blown *Demoiselle (dem wa zell) fluttered down upon the blue pond next.

Her gentle landing, or course, caused Le S. Elf to become

all...blow-bubbly, vexed.

The shimmering glory of her rainbowed wings

Did not cause the fish to think of pleasant, well-meaning things.

*Dragonfly

The worm was small.

More l...o...n...g than tall.

However, he was clever and smart.

At the VERY last instant, he made a quick dart.

You see, the worm also had his bag of tricks.

There wasn't much that worm could not fix.

With a slippery worm-wiggle,

With a super-fast worm-squiggle,

The little worm beat a very hasty retreat.

Too wise was he...

To hang around and be...

Something munchy

and crunchy...

for the fish to eat.

It was the fish that bubbled

an angry cough

When the worm was

suddenly from the hook...

off.

Le S. Elf bubble-glugged with all his might.

"Hey! I will give you such a fight.

I will give you a great big bite!"

Shark-like he circled around the worm... tight.

"This fighting fish will turn you...

into...

a real tasty worm-dish!"

Le S. Elf then opened his jaws

REAL wide.

All the better to get that

whole...

worm...

deep...

inside.

Le S. Elf was such a hostile lout.

Once again, in...HIS...pond, he swirled all about.

Then he began that same tired, old, loud, fish shout.

"Out! Out! Out! This is my pond! Of that, there can be no doubt!

Therefore, you must fly out!... Out! Out!"

Le S. Elf created such a combative hue and cry.

Away...away...sailed Demoiselle, soft as a summer sigh.

Her appreciation for peace and love were so very high.

Sad, but, in this small, blue pond they did not seem to lie.

She had her standards. She would rather do than die.

And since, with those who made war,

she would not vie,

She being more the lover...

less the fighter...oh my!

That being that...Away...away...gentle Demoiselle did fly.

A little, lame, white *Canard (can-nar) quacked a happy quack

as she waddled into the small blue pond.

You see, ducks and water have a mutual and natural bond.

They go together, like birds of a feather.

The blue pond water tickled the toes on ducks web-footed feet.

"Oh! Wonderful, wonderful water! So wet and so sweet.

Of you, dearest friend, I am so very, very fond.

I think that I shall love living here on this small, blue pond."

*Duck

Le S. Elf, in a fighting rage-double

Gave out an irritating blow-fish bubble.

That annoying sound of elf-fish trouble.

How overwhelmingly sad.

It is pitifully bad.

To be so grossly mad

That it curls a fish's fin.

What a sad...bad...mad sin

For any fish to ever fall in.

Spitting out great gobs of bubbly foam.

Raging because he wanted to be left all alone.

Making a freakish fish-squeal,

One with lots of frenzied fish-zeal.

Le S. Elf shouted...as rude...as rude could

ever think to be.

"Go worm! Go from MY sea!"

The worm squirmed. The worm turned.

The worm sighed.

"Uh-oh!"

Then the worm bravely replied,

'Well...No!"

"This pond...'Tis mine, 'Tis mine, 'Tis mine,"

Gurgled Le S. Elf with an irritating, bubbly-fish whine.

Such a fish-bully swagger.

Like a mean-mouthed bragger.

With a great deal of self-righteous anger,

Le S. Elf nipped a pretty, white feather right out of little,

lame duck's tail.

Off and away, in that web-footed waddle, hobbled duck

Through the mud and muck

With a timid "Quack" and a sad, alarmed wail.

A laughing, freckle-faced *Garconnet (gar-sewn) made a

GREAT BIG red-headed splash when he dived in.

This put Le S. Elf on the spot.

The fish was not at all that hot

About letting him, an actual, real life, human boy stay for a swim!

At first Le S. Elf tried to scare the boy with a bubble-glug fish bluff.

Then, of course, when that did not work, he got a little rough.

You see Le S. Elf always had to be the one to win.

But the boy, being a boy, would never let something with a

fin do him in.

*Boy

Le S. Elf, in a fast swirl

Did a complete, triple-turn twirl.

What a mean, unclean, monstrous rotter

The fish, all alone, had become...in the blow-bubbly water.

Swimming frantically around...and around;

Searching angrily until that *Ver (vair) on the hook he found.

*Worm

Later that very same day,

A red-headed, freckle-faced *pecheur (pesh-er) came by the way.

He dropped in his line...ker-plunk!

To the bottom of the small, blue pond it sunk.

"I can not be had.

I do not fight.

I do not get mad.

I can make it right."

The boy smiled under

his big straw hat.

"Well fish

that's....that!"

*Fisherman

"Well, look at that!

What a fish!

So big! So fat!

Fish, don't do that!

Be good.

Like a regular fish should.

Or, you could end up a fish...dish!"

Le S. Elf simply...could...not...stand it.

He really had a big, fish fit.

Le S. Elf was in such a terrible peeve.

Still...

the boy absolutely...

positively, refused to leave.

To Le S. Elf it did not seem at

all...right.

So...

he gave the boy a horrible,

nasty fish bite.

Right on...Red-head's toe.

Oh!...Oh!...Oh!

That is a...No!...No!...No!

"Oh...oh...oh...Gross fish!

It is not my wish

to kick up a water-war storm.

But that really was...in bad form."

He admonished Le S. Elf in startled surprise.

Then the offended boy, from the small, blue pond did arise.

Affirming to the fish...that...which you and I have already surmised.

"You, Mr. Fish, are a most wicked and improper grouch!"

The boy refused to utter even one little Ouch! Ouch! Ouch!

The Garconnet was not one to snivel and moan.

Bravely, clutching his wound, Red-head departed for home.

Printed in the United States
By Bookmasters